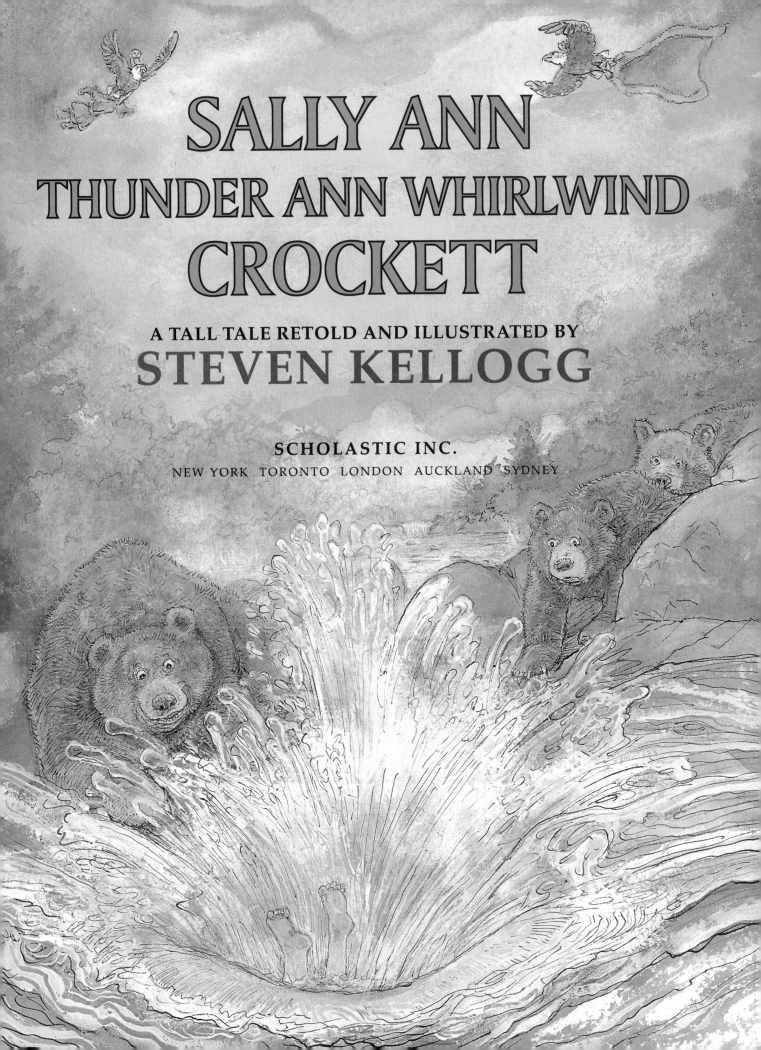

SALLY ANN
THUNDER ANN WHIRLWIND
CROCKETT

A TALL TALE RETOLD AND ILLUSTRATED BY
STEVEN KELLOGG

SCHOLASTIC INC.

NEW YORK TORONTO LONDON AUCKLAND SYDNEY

ISBN 0-590-96999-4

Copyright © 1995 by Steven Kellogg.
All rights reserved. Published by Scholastic Inc., 555 Broadway, New York, NY 10012, by arrangement with William Morrow and Company.

12 11 10 9 8 7   3 4 5 6/0

Printed in the U.S.A.   14

First Scholastic printing, September 1996

AUTHOR'S NOTE

The roots of much of America's tall-tale literature are to be found in the stories that fill the Davy Crockett almanacs, which were published from 1834 to 1856. Davy Crockett's wife has a prominent role in eight of the tales, and she is identified as Sally Ann Thunder Ann Whirlwind in the 1854 almanac adventure entitled *A Perilous Situation of Mrs. Crockett.* My picture-book version of her exploits draws from a number of the almanac tales, particularly *A Thief of an Alligator* (1836), *A Tongariferous Fight with an Alligator* (1827), *A Pretty Predicament* (1839), and *Mike Fink Trying to Scare Mrs. Crockett* (1850).

*To that heroic Emily
with love*

About two hundred years ago a remarkable infant came into the world, beaming like a sunrise. Having nine sons already, her parents were overjoyed to welcome their first daughter.

"Howdy! I'm Sally Ann Thunder Ann Whirlwind!" shouted the baby in a voice as loud as a blast of buckshot.

Her parents were astonished. "You can talk!" they cried.

"I can out-talk, out-grin, out-scream, out-swim, and out-run any baby in Kentucky!" she announced.

"You're amazing!" exclaimed her parents. Their sons, however, had been hoping for another brother, and they did not agree.

"She's a loudmouth and a liar," grumbled one brother.

"Everybody knows that babies can't run," scoffed another.

"Especially baby girls," added the oldest.

"She couldn't out-run a loaf of bread," sneered the youngest.

"I'm ready to try!" cried their sister. "Let's race to the top of the mountain and back. On your mark! Get set! GO!" Sally Ann Thunder Ann Whirlwind took off like a cheetah.

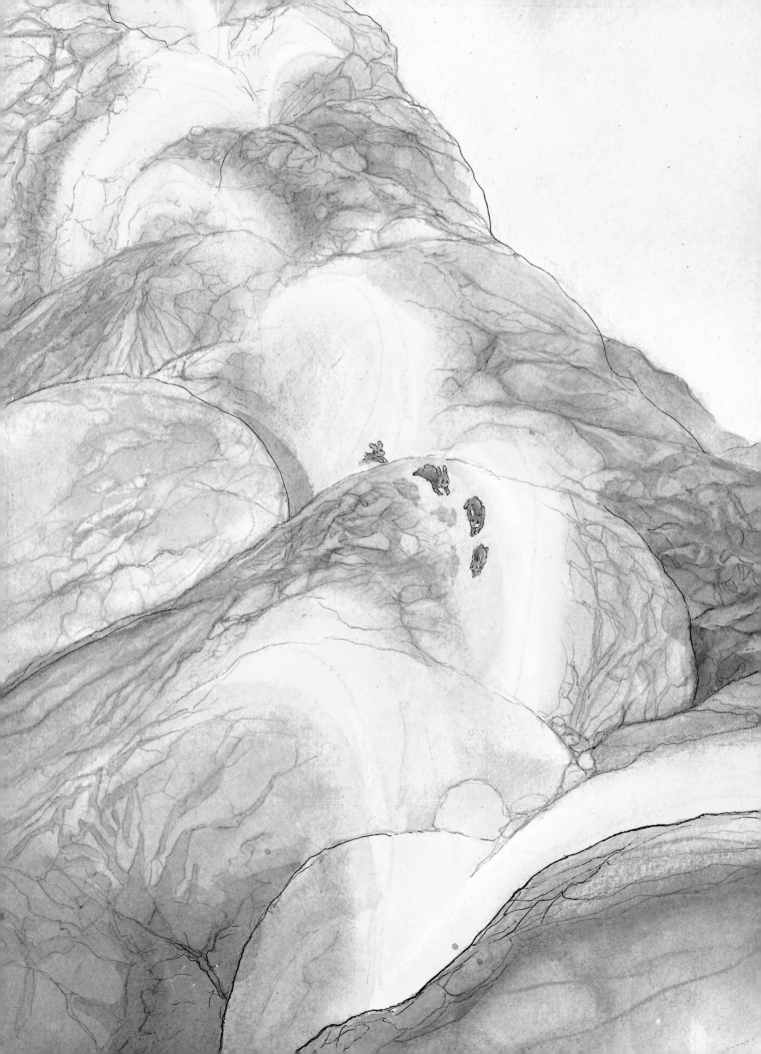

Sally Ann blazed up the mountain, shooting past a gang of racing rabbits as if they were dozing tortoises. On her way back down, she met her brothers, who were just beginning the climb. "I'll see you at the finish line!" she called.

When Sally Ann's brothers finally returned, they collapsed in the shade for a nap.

"Let's have a swimming race!" cried Sally Ann.

But her exhausted brothers had lost interest in sports. "We quit!" they cried.

Sally Ann dove underwater and went fishing with the otters.

When an hour passed and she didn't surface, her brothers became concerned. Has she drowned? they wondered.

Suddenly Sally Ann rocketed into view juggling fourteen trout.

"Grease the griddle!" she cried. "It's dinnertime!"

Sally Ann's brothers finally admitted that their parents were right. "She's amazing," they agreed.

Sally Ann continued to astonish folks throughout her childhood. When she was one year old, she beat the fastest runners in the state.

At four she flipped the strongest arm wrestlers.

At seven she was the champion tug-of-war team.

On her eighth birthday Sally Ann decided she was grown-up and ready for new challenges. "I'm off to the frontier!" she announced.

For several years she lived with different animals and learned their habits.

She loved life in the wilderness during every season
except winter.

Finally, the fierce cold drove her underground to
hibernate with the bears. Deep in a cave that bristled
with stalactites and stalagmites Sally Ann snuggled close
to a large warm grizzly.

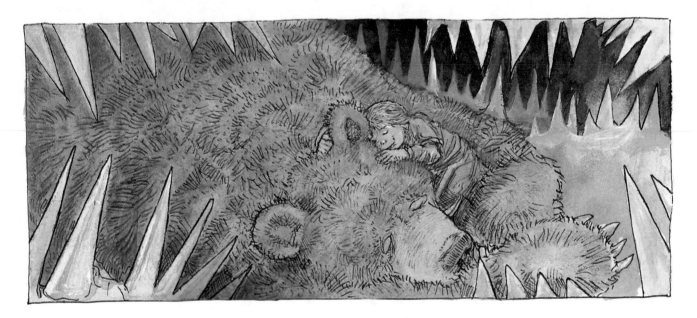

Suddenly the bear awakened, and Sally Ann felt a blast of terrible heat from his great ovenlike mouth. It was clear that the bear was more interested in a snack than a roommate.

But before the monster could swallow her, Sally Ann
stunned him with a grin as bright as a flash of lightning.

Over backward he went, rolling among razor-sharp stalactites and stalagmites that skinned him from his ears to his toes. Naked and embarrassed, the creature scrambled out of sight. "That was a close shave for both of us!" cried Sally Ann.

She wrapped herself in the bear's fur and set off in search of new adventures.

That bearskin kept Sally Ann cozy for many winters,
and she grew tall and strong. But as the years rolled by she
became tired of living alone.

One day she came upon an unhappy fellow who had dozed off while leaning against a tree and awakened to find himself stuck. Two eagles were adding to his misery by yanking out his hair to line their nests.

"You're in a pretty predicament, mister!" exclaimed Sally Ann. "Let me give you a hand."

Sally Ann tried to shoo away the eagles, but they fought her like flapping furies. So she let loose a wild scream that blasted the color off their heads and tails and left them as placid as pigeons.

"Well, star spangle my banner!" cried Sally Ann Thunder Ann Whirlwind. "I've just invented bald eagles!"

Unfortunately, the fellow Sally Ann was trying to rescue had been knocked unconscious by her scream. Quickly she hauled six rattlers out of a nearby snake den, knotted them together, and lassoed a branch. One sharp tug and his head popped free.

He's kind of handsome, thought Sally Ann. I'll freshen up and look my best before I nurse him back to health.

Sally Ann grabbed a hornet's nest for a bonnet and
fogged herself with the perfume of a passing skunk.

Then she heaved her patient into the creek.

Just as she expected, the minute he hit that icy water he perked right up. "My heart's pounding like a buffalo stampede," he sputtered.

"So's mine," confessed Sally Ann.

"My name is Davy Crockett. Marry me!" he exclaimed.

Sally Ann was astonished to learn that she had rescued the most famous woodsman in America. Lightning flashed between them, and they fell head over heels in love.

The happy couple celebrated their wedding with a
batch of eagle-egg eggnog. Then they settled down in
a farmhouse with a fine view of the Mississippi River.

When their first child, Hardstone, was born, all three of them whooped for joy. "Let's have thirty more!" cried Sally Ann Thunder Ann Whirlwind Crockett.

Not long afterward a city slicker stopped by and asked Davy if he would be willing to run in November. Thinking that a footrace was being organized, Davy replied, "Sign me up!"

Later Davy was flabbergasted to discover that he had agreed to run for the United States Congress—what's more, he'd been elected!

As soon as Davy left for Washington, D.C., Sally Ann
started having trouble with the alligators.

She hid her porkers in hollow logs, but the gators stole
the logs and the hogs.

"They'll be snatching little Hardstone next," fretted
Sally Ann.

Late the next night a gang of bull alligators surrounded the Crocketts' farmhouse.

Sally Ann awoke to a tremendous racket. Ceiling plaster
was falling, and plates leaped from the shelves.

To Sally Ann's dismay the hooligan reptiles swarmed onto her roof to play King of the Mountain. Chimneys toppled, windows shattered, and shingles scattered as the game got under way.

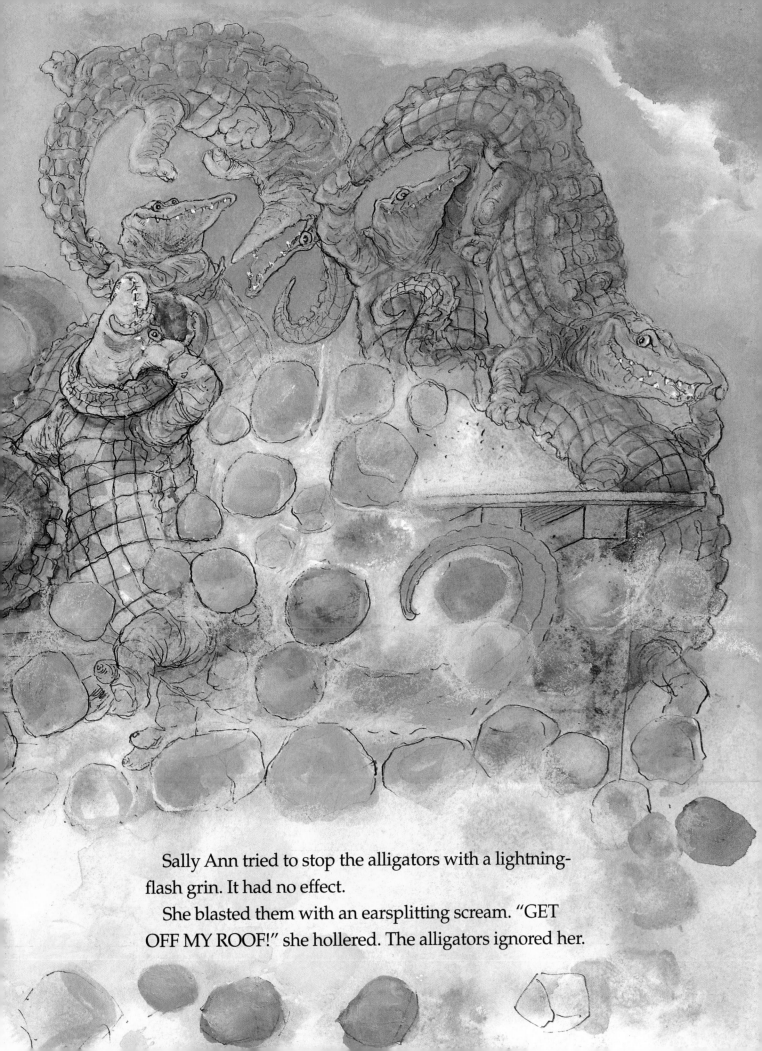

Sally Ann tried to stop the alligators with a lightning-flash grin. It had no effect.

She blasted them with an earsplitting scream. "GET OFF MY ROOF!" she hollered. The alligators ignored her.

Finally, Sally Ann flung herself into the King of the Mountain competition with such energy that she kicked up a tornado.

In a few seconds all the alligators had been blown away, and Sally Ann Thunder Ann Whirlwind Crockett stood alone as Queen of the Mountain. For the next few days it rained alligators from Minnesota to New Orleans.

When Davy Crockett returned from Congress, he was so proud of Sally Ann's heroic feat that he couldn't stop bragging. He even interrupted a wrestling match to tell the story to Mike Fink.

Now, Mike Fink was a keelboat captain as well as a champion wrestler. He had tangled with alligators up and down the Mississippi, and he couldn't believe that anyone had trounced a whole tribe of the critters at once.

Mike had his crew stitch him into an alligator hide. Then he set out to scare Sally Ann into confessing that her husband's Queen of the Mountain story was a bald-faced lie.

Mike crept up behind Sally Ann and little Hardstone.

"The King of the Mountain has arrived!" he roared.

Sally Ann whipped that alligator hide around so fast
that the stitches popped and Mike Fink was propelled
skyward.

Folks knew that every strong man in the Mississippi Valley who wrestled the mighty Mike Fink found himself thrown flat, so they were amazed to hear that Mike had been flung five miles upriver by Sally Ann Thunder Ann Whirlwind Crockett.